THE LOUD HOUSE

NO BUS, NO FUSS

SCHOLASTIC INC.

ISBN 978-1-338-84796-3

10 9 8 7 6 5 4 3 2 1   22 23 24 25 26
Printed in the U.S.A.   40

First printing 2022

Designed by Ashley Vargas

It was morning at the Loud House, and
Lincoln was running late . . . as usual.
He misplaced his backpack . . . as usual.
He stumbled out the door . . . as usual.
Lynn even stole his breakfast . . . as usual!

None of that bothered Lincoln! When the bus came, he climbed on and said hi to all his friends. "It's finally Friday—or should I say Fri-*yay*?"

His best friend Clyde laughed.

Before Lincoln could sit down next to Clyde, a spring popped out of the seat.

"I guess I'll just sit in the back to-*yay!*" Lincoln said cheerfully.

He headed to the back of the bus to drink his orange juice.

When Lincoln sat down, three eighth graders appeared.

"Why are you sitting in our seat?" one of them asked, frowning.

Lincoln looked around, confused.

"Eighth graders in the back and babies in the front," said another one of the older kids.

As Lincoln got up, the bus hit a bump. Oops! His orange juice spilled all over one of the eighth graders!

"Sorry!" Lincoln cried. "Let me get that for you." He tried to scrub the orange juice out, but he only made the stain bigger.

Lincoln's friends all tried to help.

Stella tossed him a stain-removing pen, but it turned out to be a marker.

Zach threw Lincoln his sandwich, hoping the bread would soak up the juice. But the sandwich hit the eighth grader in the face instead.

Liam tried to use cow manure as a stain remover, but that made things much, *much* worse!

By the time they got to school, Lincoln and his friends were in big trouble. The eighth graders had given them all atomic wedgies!

"Thanks for trying to help me, guys," Lincoln said. "I guess it could have gone worse."

"Speak for yourself," Rusty groaned.

The bus ride home that day didn't go any better. This time, Lincoln, Stella, Clyde, Liam, Rusty, and Zach all ended up in one huge atomic wedgie. Ouch!

"I don't have enough strength or underwear to keep riding this bus," Clyde said.

There had to be some other way to get to school!

The friends all put their heads together to think.

It was too far to walk.

Not everyone had bikes.

"What if we ask our parents to drive us?" Lincoln said. "They could each take a different day!"

Problem solved . . . right?

On Monday, Zach's parents drove them to school in a van marked "Nothing to See Here Cleaners." Inside, the van was filled with charts, maps, and blinking lights. Zach's parents were actually alien hunters!

"Keep your voices down!" Zach's mom said to the kids. "You'll scare away the alien life-form!"

The van moved super slowly down the street,
following a dog wearing a cone around its neck.
"Zach, can you do something?" Stella whispered.
"We're gonna be late!"
"I think my parents might be onto something,
though," Zach said, pointing to the little dog.
Everyone groaned.

On Tuesday, Liam's Mee-Maw drove them to school on a tractor.

All of the kids squeezed into the back with some chickens, goats, and pigs. This wasn't the kind of ride any of them had in mind. What a smelly mess!

"Uh-oh!" Liam cried. "Pull over, Mee-Maw! Virginia's getting car sick again!"

Before anyone could stop her, Virginia the pig threw up on Clyde's shirt. Yuck!

"Never mind," Liam said as the pig gave a big smile. "She's doing better!"

On Wednesday, Rusty's dad drove the kids to
school in his small, crowded car. The car was
packed with racks of clothes to sell.

"A potential sale!" Rusty's dad said, spotting
a man on the street. He stopped the car and
hopped out. "Grab a rack of clothes, and don't
take no for an answer!"

Before Rusty's dad walked up to his new customer, he sprayed a huge cloud of smelly cologne. All the kids started coughing from the stench.

Rusty and his dad showed the customer clothes. The rest of the kids just kept coughing and trying to escape from the cologne smell. Pee-yew!

On Thursday, Clyde's dad drove the kids to school in his car. He was all about safety, so they had to wear life vests and were surrounded by pillows.

"Can't be too careful!" Clyde's dad said.

The kids could hardly move a muscle!

"Dad, are we ever going to go?" Clyde asked,
strapped in tight.

His dad smiled. "Just one last safety precaution!"
He covered the car in bubble wrap, then drove
slowly and carefully down the street.

The kids groaned.

On Friday, Lincoln's mom drove the kids to school in Vanzilla.

"Finally, one normal ride!" Lincoln said. What a relief!

Everything was going fine until another car cut in front of Lincoln's mom in the drop-off line.

Lincoln's mom honked her horn and yelled out the window. "Oh! Please go ahead, Your Majesty!"

Grumpy, she sped ahead and cut off a different car . . . which belonged to Mr. Bolhofner, Lincoln's teacher!

Lincoln sank in his seat. "Oh, great."

At lunch that day, the kids were glum.

"Carpooling was a bust," Zach said.

"There must be another way to get to school," Stella added.

Everyone thought hard.

Suddenly, Clyde cried out, "I've got it! We take the city bus!"

The next week, Lincoln and his friends put their new plan into action.

They waited at the city bus stop, studying the complicated map. They would need to take a few different buses, but they had it figured out. This was going to be a piece of cake!

The bus ride was an adventure!

Zach couldn't reach the passenger handle.

Clyde didn't have the right amount of money to pay for his fare.

They had to transfer from one bus to another to another . . . to another.

Finally, the group made it to the last bus.

"Guys, we did it!" Lincoln cheered. "I think this bus takes us right to school!"

Just then, a ship's horn sounded. The kids all looked out the window.

Their bus had boarded a ferry and was heading across Lake Michigan! Whoops!

The next morning, Lincoln had a new plan.
The group met at Flip's Food and Fuel. Flip was
an old man with an even older biplane!
Everyone put on helmets and goggles and
climbed into the plane. This didn't seem like
a great idea—but they had to get to school
somehow!

"Fasten your seat belts!" Flip cried.

Some seat belts were too loose. Some were too tight. Lincoln's seat belt was a garden hose.

Once the plane got into the air, everyone relaxed for a moment.

"Okay, aim for those shrubs!" Flip yelled.

What?!

Flip handed each kid a parachute before ejecting them from the plane!

Everyone screamed on the way down, but they all landed safely in a tree near the school.

"This plan stinks worse than Rusty's dad's cologne," Zach said.

Lincoln sighed. "This afternoon, we'll have to get back on the school bus."

Once they untangled themselves from the tree, Lincoln and his friends walked to the front of the school. The buses were just pulling up.

The eighth graders climbed off the bus, laughing.

Some other kids followed behind. They had atomic wedgies!

"Ever since you guys stopped taking the bus, they started picking on the rest of us," one of the kids explained.

Liam frowned. "Well, I guess it's our turn again."

But Lincoln had an idea. Maybe it didn't have to be anybody's turn!

That afternoon, Lincoln climbed on the bus and headed to the back.

The eighth graders laughed. "Babies in the front!"

"No!" Lincoln said. "You can't tell me where to sit anymore."

All of the kids on the bus stood up.

"We're tired of being bullied by you," Clyde said.

Stella nodded. "And together, we don't have to be afraid anymore."

Slowly, the eighth graders shrugged and sat
down. They were outnumbered!

The rest of the kids all cheered and high-fived.
Lincoln and his friends had stood up to the
bullies—and won!

Made in the U.S.A. PO# 5084365 06/22